Crazy
Mixed-Up
Valentines

Other Young Yearling books you will enjoy:

Monsters in the Outfield, *Stephen Mooser*
My Halloween Boyfriend, *Stephen Mooser*
Monster Holiday, *Stephen Mooser*
The Fright-Face Contest, *Stephen Mooser*
That's So Funny, I Forgot to Laugh, *Stephen Mooser*
The Mystery of the Blue Ring, *Patricia Reilly Giff*
The Riddle of the Red Purse, *Patricia Reilly Giff*
The Secret at the Polk Street School, *Patricia Reilly Giff*
The Powder Puff Puzzle, *Patricia Reilly Giff*
The Case of the Cool-Itch Kid, *Patricia Reilly Giff*
Garbage Juice for Breakfast, *Patricia Reilly Giff*
Grumpy Pumpkins, *Judy Delton*

YEARLING BOOKS/YOUNG YEARLINGS/YEARLING CLASSICS are designed especially to entertain and enlighten young people. Patricia Reilly Giff, consultant to this series, received the bachelor's degree from Marymount College. She holds the master's degree in history from St. John's University, and a Professional Diploma in Reading from Hofstra University. She was a teacher and reading consultant for many years, and is the author of numerous books for young readers.

For a complete listing of all Yearling titles, write to:
Dell Readers Service
P.O. Box 1045
South Holland, IL 60473.

THE
CREEPY
CREATURE
CLUB

Crazy Mixed-Up Valentines

---◆---

Stephen Mooser

Illustrated by George Ulrich

A YOUNG YEARLING BOOK

Published by
Dell Publishing
a division of
Bantam Doubleday Dell Publishing Group, Inc.
666 Fifth Avenue
New York, New York 10103

ISBN: 0-440-40269-7

Printed in the United States of America

February 1990

10 9 8 7 6 5 4 3 2 1

W

For Bebe Willoughby,
who gave the Creepy Creature Club
a poke and helped bring it to life.

Contents

———— ◆ ————

Chapter 1

◆

Roses Are Red

Monday morning. School had just begun. But already Henry Potter was sweating. He was working on a valentine poem and it had to be perfect.

Roses are red, violets are blue, it began. *Gum balls are sweet. And so are you.*

Henry stretched his long legs under his desk and read over the words while he chewed on his thumb.

"It's good," he said to himself. "But not good enough. Not for Rosa."

Valentine's Day was coming on Friday. Everyone in Ms. Hatfield's class at the River City School was making Valentine's cards.

1

Henry was working on his extra hard. That's because it was for Rosa Dorado. He wanted her to be his valentine.

Rosa had long black hair and big brown eyes. She sat right across the aisle. Henry patted down the back of his hair. As usual it was sticking up, like a feather.

"Ah," he said, dreaming, "if Rosa would be my valentine I'd be the happiest boy in school. Maybe in the whole world."

As the students worked, their teacher, Ms. Hatfield, walked around the room. Quietly, she prowled the aisles in her Monday tennis shoes. Black-and-white ones. High tops.

"Valentine's is one of my favorite holidays," she said. "Love is in the air! Cupid is on the wing!"

Melvin Purdy raised his hand. "Who's Cupid?"

Ms. Hatfield peered over her glasses. "Why, Cupid was the Roman god of love," she said. "He would shoot his little arrow into someone's heart and make them fall in love."

Rosa put her hand to her mouth and giggled.

"Ah," said Ms. Hatfield, staring off, "I remember when I was little, we used to ..."

Henry rolled his eyes. Ms. Hatfield was always remembering. She was always talking about life when she was little.

That was fine for her. But he had work to do. Poetry needed to be written. Back to work he went.

Finally, after six more tries, he came up with something he liked.

Roses are red, violets are blue. Valentines are special. And so are you.

"That's it!" he said, squeezing his pencil. "That's the poem that's going to make Rosa my valentine."

Valentine's Day was extra special for Henry. That's because it was also his birthday. On Friday the Creepy Creature Club was having a Valentine's party at their clubhouse. He would be there. And so would Rosa.

Henry reached into his back pocket. He took out an old crinkly picture that he had clipped from a magazine. It showed a birthday party. A boy was blowing out the candles on a big chocolate cake. Behind him all his friends were clapping and singing. Underneath the picture were the words *The Happiest Birthday Ever.* Henry sighed. He had never had a birthday party like the one in the picture. His parties had always been small. Just a few friends had come.

Henry sneaked a peek at Rosa. He was hoping this year's party would be different. "If Rosa says she'll be my valentine, then I'll be just like the boy in the picture. I'll have the happiest birthday ever."

Like Henry, Rosa was a member of the Creepy Creature Club. It was a club for people who liked scary things. They collected monster cards. They went to scary movies. And they even had a clubhouse decorated like a haunted house. It was in Rosa's garage.

Henry looked across the aisle at Rosa. She was making a valentine card too. As she wrote she chewed on a bit of her long black hair. Henry sighed and dreamed about Valentine's Day. He would have a big chocolate birthday cake. It would be shaped

like a heart. Rosa would be singing to him, happy birthday to you.

Suddenly Billy Hayes snapped Henry out of his dream. "Valentines are special. And so are you," he said, talking through his nose. Henry looked up. Billy had been looking over his shoulder. "I bet I know who your valentine is for."

Henry covered his poem with his hand. He glanced across the aisle. Rosa was looking right at him. His face turned as red as a ripe strawberry. "Bug off," he mumbled. "Valentines are private."

Billy had a long, skinny neck and bushy brown eyebrows. He was wearing a goofy orange cap, turned sideways. He kept talking through his nose. "I know who you like," he sang. Then, giggling, he walked away.

"What a busybody," Henry muttered. "Well, if he likes my valentines so much, then he can have one."

And in two minutes Henry had a new valentine all written. It said: *Roses are red. Violets are blue. Noses smell. And so do you!*

Billy was up at the front talking to Ms. Hatfield. As they spoke Billy fanned himself with his hat, even though it wasn't hot.

"What a goofball," thought Henry.

Henry smiled and folded the new valentine in half. Then he put it in a little white envelope.

"I can hardly wait for him to get this," he said. "It's not going to be the valentine he wants. But it will be the one he deserves."

Chapter 2

◆

Little Cupid

When lunchtime came everyone left their valentines on their desks. Everyone but Henry. He took the envelopes with him. As he was heading down the hall he saw his friend Melvin Purdy. Melvin was the littlest member of the Creepy Creature Club. He had big ears and a little nose. On that day he was wearing striped pants. They barely reached his ankles.

Henry waved the valentine envelopes in Melvin's face. "I'm taking my valentines with me. I don't want anyone to see my cards. I don't want them stealing my poems."

"Who would want to steal your poems?" asked Melvin.

Henry chuckled. "Lots of people." They

8

turned a corner and headed for the open door to the cafeteria. "Everyone knows I'm the best poet in class."

"You're only the biggest bragger in class," said Melvin. He giggled. He thought Henry's bragging was funny. Everyone did.

"Laugh now. But someday I'll be famous," said Henry. He stuck out his chin. "I'll be on TV and everything."

"Maybe someday you will," said Melvin. "Spaghetti."

"Huh?" said Henry. He had been dreaming about being famous. "What did you say?"

"We're having spaghetti," said Melvin. He sniffed. "I can already smell it."

There were lots of things that Melvin wasn't very good at. But there was one thing he was great at: smelling. His nose may have been tiny. But it was an excellent sniffer.

Henry and Melvin walked into the cafeteria. As always, it was bright and crowded and noisy inside. And on this day it also smelled, like spaghetti.

Mrs. Ames, the cook, was already in the

9

Valentine's Day spirit. She was wearing a big plastic heart on her white cook's hat. The heart said BE MY COOKIE!

"Happy Valentine's week," said Mrs. Ames. She hummed as she dished out the spaghetti. "Cupid is on the wing!"

"That's what we've heard," said Melvin.

"We're watching out for him," said Henry. He laughed. Then he and Melvin took their trays to a nearby table and sat down.

Henry ate spaghetti like a vacuum cleaner. Face next to the plate, he'd shovel it in with a fork.

"This is a big week!" he said, pausing between bites. Three or four strings of spaghetti were still hanging out of his mouth. *Slurp!* They disappeared. "It's the biggest week of the year, in fact."

"I know," said Melvin. "It's Valentine's. On Friday the club is having a party."

Henry sucked up some more spaghetti. It wriggled its way into his mouth like a herd of worms. "Something even more important than Valentine's is happening on Friday. Even more important than the party."

10

Melvin wrinkled his brow. "It's not Halloween, is it? Or the Fourth of July?"

"No, of course not," said Henry.

"Christmas? New Year's?"

"No, silly. It's my birthday!" said Henry. He leaned across the table. He grinned. "I'm a Valentine's boy!"

Melvin had a dot of spaghetti sauce on his chin. His little eyes got round as pancakes. "A birthday! What kind of presents are you going to get?"

"I don't know," said Henry. "What are you going to get me?"

Melvin rubbed his fist against his cheek. "Sorry," he said. "I don't have any money."

Henry looked around the crowded cafeteria. He saw Rosa a few tables over. She was sitting next to red-haired Ginger Stein. They were giggling about something. Billy Hayes was sitting at the end of the same table. He was with the Sharks. The Sharks were a gang of bullies. Most of the time the Sharks and the Creepy Creatures didn't get along. Twice they had almost gotten in fights. Suddenly, Henry remembered the Valentine's cards.

11

"Melvin! I know what you can give me for a present," he said. He reached across the table and patted his friend's hand. "You can be my mailman."

Melvin tilted his head. "Huh?"

"I need your help," said Henry. He looked around to make sure no one was listening. Then he lowered his voice. "I want you to deliver some valentines. One goes to Rosa. The other one goes to Billy."

"Sure," said Melvin. "But why do you need me? Can't you deliver them yourself?"

Henry chewed on his thumb. "I guess I could give Billy his, but not Rosa's. No way. I'd be afraid."

Melvin wrinkled his brow. "Big, brave Henry Potter is afraid? I don't believe it. You're always bragging that nothing scares you."

"Monsters don't scare me. Snakes don't scare me. Bullies don't scare me. But I get scared asking someone to be my valentine, especially Rosa." Henry lowered his voice. "So please. You talk for me. Deliver my valentine to Rosa."

"You mean I get to play Cupid?" he said.

Henry blushed. "I guess that's what you would be."

"Cupid! The Roman god of love, wow!" Melvin beamed. He sat back in his chair and folded his arms across his chest. "It would be fun to be somebody famous. Especially someone as nice as Cupid." He smiled. "Sure. I'll deliver your valentines."

Henry got out the two envelopes. He looked around the cafeteria again. Then he passed them to Melvin. "Okay, now. The big one goes to Rosa. And the little one is for Billy. Got it?"

Melvin stood up. He touched the valentines to his forehead in a little salute. "Don't worry. I'm going to be a perfect Cupid."

"Then wipe that spaghetti sauce off your chin," said Henry. "Cupid doesn't have half a lunch on his face."

Melvin wiped off the sauce.Then he stood at attention and saluted again. "Ready, sir. Cupid is about to take wing."

"Don't crash," said Henry. "I'm counting on you."

Melvin winked. "Don't worry. Cupid knows what to do."

Henry watched Melvin walk over to where Rosa was sitting. He tapped Rosa on the shoulder. When Rosa turned around, he bowed low. Then he handed her the card.

"For me?" she said, putting her hand on her heart. She blushed and looked around.

Henry gave her a little wave and she smiled. Then, while she was opening the envelope, Melvin walked over to Billy. He tapped Billy on the shoulder. Then handed him the envelope.

"What's this?" said Billy.

"It's from Henry," said Melvin. "Your secret admirer."

Billy looked at the envelope. Then across the way at Henry.

Henry stood up and pointed at Billy. "Open it up!" he said in a loud voice. "And find out what I think of you!"

Billy shrugged his shoulders. He opened the envelope. By now everyone was looking. The Sharks crowded around. They wanted to see what the valentine said.

Henry folded his arms across his chest and waited. Suddenly, the Sharks began hooting and whistling. And Billy's face got red.

"I hope I embarrassed him good," said Henry.

Henry looked over at Rosa. Her face was red too. But not with embarrassment. With anger. She stood up and pointed across the cafeteria at Henry.

"I think you smell too!" she said. "Like a skunk with bad breath!"

Henry gulped. Could the cards have gotten mixed up?

"Henry loves Billy! Henry loves Billy!" chanted the Sharks. They poked Billy in the back and whistled. "Oooo-eee!"

Now it was Henry's turn to be embarrassed.

"Rosa!" he said, holding out his arms, begging. "Please. There's been a mistake."

"There certainly has!" Rosa shouted back. "The mistake was thinking you and I were friends!"

Cupid came scurrying back. "I don't think love is on the wing, is it?"

Henry growled. "No! But you're going to be." He made a fist. "Some Cupid. I'd like to send you back in time, where you belong."

"Mistakes happen," said Melvin.

"You mixed up the valentines," said Henry. "Thanks a lot."

"It's your fault too," said Melvin. "You should have done it yourself. If you hadn't been such a chicken, this never would have happened."

Melvin's words stopped Henry cold. He chewed on his thumb and thought.

"I hate to admit it, but you're right," he said. He looked over at Rosa. She was still glaring at him. "I'm so embarrassed. Now Rosa thinks I told her she smells. She'll never be my valentine now. Never."

Chapter 3

♦

Cupid Strikes Again

Tuesday was gym day. Henry brought a change of socks to school. After gym he put his dirty socks in a paper bag. Then he put the bag under his desk.

As soon as he spotted Melvin Purdy, he made a face.

Melvin rubbed his fist against his cheek. "Sorry," he said.

The rest of the class was still coming into the room. Ms. Hatfield was up at the board. She was drawing hearts in the corners.

Melvin tucked his chin into his shoulder. Then he walked over to Henry's desk. He had a paper bag in his hand. And a little paper heart pinned to his shirt. There was an arrow through the heart. Around the edges was written, *Hi! Call me Cupid!*

"I brought something for you," he said. "To make up for yesterday."

Henry sighed and took the bag. "It better be something pretty good."

When Henry looked inside he saw a candy heart. It was wrapped in shiny red paper.

"My mom gave me the money to buy it," said Melvin.

"Thank you," said Henry. He licked his lips. "You got this for me?"

"For you to give to Rosa," said Melvin. "So she'll be your valentine." He patted his paper heart. "Look. I made myself the class Cupid. I'm going to help everyone find a valentine."

Henry smiled. "Who's going to be your valentine?"

Melvin nodded toward the little red-haired girl in the back of the class. She was making a cat's cradle with some string. Melvin lowered his voice. "I'm going to ask Ginger

19

Stein. She'll have to say yes to Cupid." He blushed. "I hope."

"I wish I knew what Rosa was going to say," said Henry. "I'm afraid she's going to say no. I think she's still mad about the mixed-up valentines."

"She won't say no if you give her the heart," said Melvin. He waved a finger in Henry's face. "Take it from Cupid. Chocolate hearts work every time."

"They better," said Henry. "If she said no I'd be so embarrassed. I'd have to leave town."

"Better not wait too long," said Melvin. "You don't want someone else to ask first."

"Who else might ask?" said Henry.

"I don't know. Billy Hayes, maybe. I think he might like Rosa," said Melvin.

Henry gulped. "Do you think he's asked her yet?"

"I don't think so," said Melvin. "But you better not wait too long."

"I won't," said Henry. "I'll give Rosa the candy heart at lunch." He patted Melvin on the arm. "Thanks, Cupid. You're a real pal."

Melvin looked down at his little paper heart. "Just doing my job," he said. He felt warm all over. "Being Cupid is so much fun," he said to himself. "I love getting people to like each other."

Just then Rosa walked into the room. Quickly, Henry stuffed the heart back in the bag. Then he put the sack back under his seat.

"Good morning, class!" said Ms. Hatfield, clapping her hands. "Happy three-days-before-Valentine's!"

"Good morning," said the class.

"Isn't Valentine's a wonderful time," she said. "It's a time when everyone is thinking about the people that they like. That's nice." She sighed and stared out the window. "Why, I remember the first valentine I ever received from a boy. His name was Dan Thompson and ..." Ms. Hatfield was off and daydreaming again.

Henry looked over at Rosa and smiled. Rosa looked back and stuck out her tongue.

"Rosa," he whispered, starting to explain about the mixed-up valentines. But before he could finish, Ms. Hatfield had stopped dreaming. And she was peering over her glasses in his direction.

"Henry, tell us why Friday is a such a special day for you," she asked.

"That's easy," said Henry. "It's my birth-day!"

Ms. Hatfield put her hand to her cheek. "Oh, my, a Valentine's boy."

Henry looked around the room. He patted down his feather of hair. "Hint, hint," he said. "I hope everyone buys me a present."

Everyone laughed.

"Okay, then. Hint, hint. Give me a party," he said. Henry thought about the picture in his pocket. That's the kind of party he wanted, the happiest birthday ever.

Ms. Hatfield smiled. "I bet it's hard to be a Valentine's boy," she said. "It would be like having your birthday on Christmas. In all the excitement people might forget your special day."

"That's right," said Henry. He looked over at Rosa. "So hint, hint. Don't forget me."

"I'm sorry. I don't think I know you," said Rosa, scratching her head.

Henry's face turned red. Everyone laughed.

Henry chewed on his thumb, then sneaked a peek under his desk. He needed lunch to come. Fast. The sooner he could give Rosa the candy heart, the better. Then they could be friends again. And she could be his valentine.

The morning dragged by. Ms. Hatfield spent half the time talking about subtraction. The rest of the time she talked about all the Valentine's Days she could remember.

Ten o'clock crept by. Then eleven came, slow as a snail. Finally it was eleven-thirty. Then, at last, it was noon.

BRRRRING! Everyone leapt out of their seats and headed for lunch.

Henry scooped up the bag under his desk. He peeked inside and looked at the little red heart.

"I'll run by and drop this on Rosa's table in the cafeteria. "When she sees it she'll get the message for sure. She'll know I want her to be my valentine."

Henry was barely out the door when he felt a hand on his shoulder. He spun around.

It was Billy Hayes. As always, he was wearing his silly cap, turned sideways.

"Don't trick me like that again," he said. "The Sharks are still laughing at me."

Henry took Billy's hand off his shoulder. "That valentine wasn't meant for you," he said. "Melvin messed up."

Billy narrowed his eyes. "Then you don't really like me?"

"Me like a Shark? No way!" said Henry. "Even Valentine's Day couldn't make us friends."

Billy wiped his brow. "Whew!" he said. "Am I glad to hear you say that. I didn't want you for a valentine. I want someone else."

Henry raised an eyebrow. "Who do you want?"

"Valentines are private," said Billy. He started talking through his nose. "You said so yourself."

Then he took off his cap and bowed. "See you later," he said in that same silly voice.

Henry watched him walk away. "What a

goofball," he said. "I hope Rosa chooses me instead of him."

When Henry got to the cafeteria he saw Billy talking to his friends the Sharks. Zack Morton, the head of the Sharks, was on one side of him and Angie Dobbs was on the other. Angie had long dirty brown hair and a tiny freckled nose. She was poking Billy in the side and laughing.

"What a goofball she is," said Henry. "Just like Billy."

The sound of rattling trays and chattering students filled the air. So did the smell of tuna fish. Henry looked around for Rosa. He saw her at last, sitting near the wall, talking to Ginger. While she listened to something Ginger was saying she chewed on a strand of her long black hair. Henry sighed. Even with that hair in her mouth she looked like the prettiest girl in school.

"I'll give Rosa the heart after lunch," said Henry, getting into the cafeteria line. "I'll wait till she's all alone. Why hurry? Anyway, I need time to practice what I'm going to say."

Mrs. Ames gave Henry a tuna-fish sandwich and some french fries. On her hat she was wearing a new valentine heart. This one said: YOU'RE MY HOT POTATO.

While Henry was searching for a place to sit he spotted Melvin Purdy strolling into the cafeteria. Melvin was wearing a too-big sweatshirt and a silly grin. When he spotted Henry he waved and held up a wrinkled paper bag.

"Melvin must be helping out someone else," said Henry. He looked down at the bag on his tray, the one with the chocolate heart. "I feel sorry for whoever he's helping out. He'll probably mess up again."

Melvin pointed to his bag. Then to the heart on his shirt.

Henry wrinkled his brow. "What's he trying to say?" he wondered. The bag in Melvin's hand looked familiar. But Henry couldn't remember where he had seen it before.

Melvin wove his way through the cafeteria. He was heading for Rosa.

When Rosa saw Melvin coming, she looked up. Melvin bowed low and said loudly, "Cupid brings greetings from a friend."

Rosa looked at Ginger and giggled.

"Cupid?" she said.

Melvin pointed to his paper heart. "Me!"

Henry set down his tray and waited to see what would happen.

Melvin held out the bag. "I bring you a present from Henry Potter. It's just a little something to let you know how he feels."

Rosa took a long look at the bag. She raised an eyebrow. "Is this another one of Henry's jokes?"

"Not this time," said Melvin. "I promise."

Rosa took the bag. "This better not be a trick."

"It's not. It's just Henry's special way of saying what he thinks of you." Melvin smiled. "Go on. Open it up."

Rosa put her hand to her mouth. She blushed. "Something special? For me?"

Everyone at the table went, "Aaahh, how nice."

"What kind of a present is he bringing from me?" wondered Henry. "I didn't give him anything for Rosa."

Rosa stuck her hand in the bag. "I'm going to give Henry a second chance."

"Oh, no!" said Henry. All at once he remembered where he had seen the bag before.

"Yeeeeee . . . yikes!" screamed Rosa. Her hand came out of the bag, holding Henry's dirty socks. "Yuck!"

"Oh, gross," said Ginger, making a face.

"Whoops!" said Melvin.

Everyone was laughing at Rosa. She let the socks fall onto the table. Then she searched the room for Henry. He was standing just one table away, his hands raised in the air.

"Rosa. It's a mistake," he said.

Rosa growled. "So this is how you feel about me? Are you trying to say I'm like your dirty socks?"

Henry thought he might faint. Suddenly he remembered the candy heart. "Wait!" he said. "I . . ."

But it was too late. Rosa was too embarrassed to stay another second in the cafeteria. Everyone was laughing at her. Out the door she ran, red-faced and nearly in tears.

Henry stomped over to Melvin. He put his hands on his hips.

"Some Cupid," he said. "What's wrong with you? Why did you give her my socks?"

Melvin rubbed his fist against his cheek. "Sorry," he said. "I saw the bag under your desk. I thought you forgot the heart. I brought it to the cafeteria so that I could play Cupid."

Henry reached out and tore the paper heart off Melvin's shirt.

"Cupid! You're fired," he said.

Melvin looked as if he was going to cry. "Does this mean you don't like me?"

"Cabbagehead! Ding-dong!" said Henry. "You're the worst Cupid ever. Don't ever do me a favor again. Understand?"

Melvin rubbed his fist against his cheek. "Don't worry." He sniffled. "I wouldn't help you for a zillion bucks. From now on talk for yourself. Just see how easy it is, big, brave Henry Potter."

"Don't worry, I will," said Henry.

Melvin sniffled again. Getting people to like each other was turning out to be harder than he had thought. He couldn't even get anyone to like him.

Chapter 4

◆

Party Plans

After school the Creepy Creatures met at their clubhouse in Rosa's garage. There was lots of work to be done. Decorations had to be made for the Valentine's Day party.

Henry got to the clubhouse late. Six or seven bikes were already leaning against the garage wall.

Henry drew in a deep breath. He had a lot of explaining to do. He hoped Rosa would understand.

He stepped to the door. He knocked.

"Who's there?" came a squeaky voice from the other side.

"Mummy," said Henry, giving the secret password.

"Mummy who?"

"Mummy, is Daddy home yet?" said Henry.

"Come in!" said Rosa, opening the door. But when she saw Henry she frowned. "I hope you don't have any more dirty laundry for me."

Henry shook his head and patted down his wild feather of hair.

"Henry, you're late," said Rosa. "We've got lots of work to do. We're making decorations for the party."

Henry looked out into the clubhouse. Everyone was busy. Ginger Stein was sitting on a long green couch, blowing up red balloons. Melvin Purdy was making a scary Valentine's poster. It read: DRACULA SAYS, BE MY VALENTINE. I WANT YOUR HEART. AND YOUR NECK! Other Creepy Creatures were hanging up streamers and cutting hearts out of red paper. Above all this, twisting slowly, was a big rubber spider. Someone had taped a plastic heart to his legs.

"Ginger needs a break," said Rosa. "Go

down to the couch and start blowing up balloons."

Henry's mouth flopped open. "What? You want me to blow up balloons? That would be a waste of my talent."

Rosa scrunched up her face. "What talent?"

"As an artist. Everyone knows I'm the best artist in school. Maybe in the whole world," said Henry. "I should be in charge of drawing pictures. Why do I have to blow up balloons?"

"Because you have the biggest mouth," said Rosa. "That's why."

"Ha-ha," said Henry. "Very funny."

"I'm sorry," said Rosa, "but everyone has to help. We want to have the best Valentine's Day party ever."

"Hint, hint," said Henry. He wiggled a finger in Rosa's face. "Don't forget there's something else to celebrate on Friday."

"Like what?" said Rosa.

"Like my birthday, of course," said Henry. "Chocolate cake is my favorite thing to eat. And a monster book is my favorite present to get." He wiggled his eyebrows some more. "Hint, hint."

35

"Sorry," said Rosa. "Your birthday is not as important as Valentine's Day."

"Well, it is to me," said Henry. He made a sad face and thought about the picture in his pocket, the happiest birthday ever. He was beginning to think he was never going to have a big birthday party like other people had.

Rosa sighed. "I have to get back to work. Go down and start blowing up those balloons."

Henry nodded. He couldn't let Rosa get away. He had to ask her the big question. Now.

"Rosa," he said. "I was wondering . . ."

"Wondering what?" asked Rosa.

"Rosa . . . I—I . . ." Henry tugged on his chin. But the words just wouldn't come out.

Rosa tilted her head.

"Yes?" she said.

Henry drew in a deep breath. "Rosa. I—I . . ." Six little words: *Rosa, will you be my valentine?* Why couldn't he say them?

Rosa put a hand to her ear. "Yes, Henry. What is it?"

Henry gulped and looked around the clubhouse. Ginger was looking right at him. So was nearly everyone else.

Henry felt weak. "Rosa. Will you . . ."

Rosa leaned forward. She was beginning to get angry. "Speak up! Will you what?"

Henry looked over his shoulder at the door. For a moment he thought about escaping. "Melvin, I'm sorry I yelled at you," he whispered to himself. "Save me, Cupid. Please. I need you."

Henry turned back to Rosa. Next to her was a poster of a wart-faced zombie. Not far away the spider swung slowly from the ceiling. But even in such ugly company Henry thought Rosa looked beautiful.

Rosa put a strand of her hair in her mouth and chewed. "What's wrong?" she mumbled. "Is there something wrong with me?"

Henry looked around the clubhouse. Why did everyone have to be looking! No way could he say the words.

"I got to go," he finally said. "I'll see you around."

"What?" said Rosa. She let the hair fall

out of her mouth. "But, Henry, we need your big mouth. Those balloons won't blow up by themselves."

Henry threw up his hands. He began backing toward the door. "My mom needs me," he said. "I forgot."

Rosa put her hands on her hips. Her brown eyes flashed. "Don't bother to come back," she said. "I'm serious. We'll put on the party without you."

Henry was in a daze. He had to get outside. He threw open the door and dashed into the cool afternoon air. Rosa shouted something after him, but he didn't hear what it was.

He ran all the way home. Big, brave Henry. The biggest mouth in the school. Maybe in the whole world. And he couldn't say six little words.

Chapter 5

◆

Creamed Spinach

Usually Henry was a very happy person. In fact, he liked to brag that he was the happiest person in the world.

But he didn't feel very happy as he ran home that afternoon. He wasn't happy that night either. His mom noticed it right away.

"Henry, what's wrong?" she asked as they were sitting at the dinner table. "You're not eating your creamed spinach."

"I'm sorry," he said. "I'm not hungry."

Mrs. Potter studied him a long time through her fancy glasses. They were big and round. Fake diamonds circled the edges.

"Something must be very wrong if you

39

won't touch your creamed spinach," she said.

Most kids hated creamed spinach. But Henry loved it. Usually.

"Is something wrong at school?" asked his mom.

Henry stared down at his plate. "It's Rosa," he mumbled.

"Rosa Dorado?" said Mrs. Potter. Her hair was twisted around the top of her head like a towel. "Rosa seems like such a sweet girl. Has she been mean to you?"

"No. Not at all," said Henry. "I want her to be my valentine."

"Then why don't you ask her, dear?" said Mrs. Potter. She patted her hair. She was always patting her hair, just like Henry.

Henry played with his spinach. "Asking Rosa isn't that easy. I don't know what to say."

Mrs. Potter smiled. "You say, 'Rosa, will you be my valentine?' "

"But what if she says no?" said Henry, looking up. "I'd be so embarrassed. It would be easier if I had someone to ask for me. Someone like Melvin. He's Cupid this week."

40

"Well, then, why not ask Melvin to help you out?" said Mrs. Potter.

Henry smoothed down his hair. "I can't. We had a fight. Now he's mad at me."

"That's probably just as well," said Mrs. Potter. She reached across the table and patted Henry on the hand. "You need to learn to speak up for yourself. Be brave. Rosa will like you better if you are."

"You really think so?" said Henry.

"I know so," said Henry's mom. "Speak for yourself. That's a good rule. You know you have a birthday coming up. Let's invite Rosa over for cake and ice cream."

Henry sighed. He rubbed his back pocket and thought about his special picture. "I wish I could have a big birthday party. Just once," he said.

Mrs. Potter nodded. "I understand. But everyone will be at the clubhouse. They always are on Valentine's Day."

"Maybe next year," said Henry. "A big chocolate cake and lots of friends. That's my wish."

"And my wish is that you would eat your spinach," said Henry's mom.

"I am a little hungry. Maybe I'll just have a bite," said Henry. Talking to his mom had helped. He felt better already. He dipped his spoon into the green gooey mush. Then he took a bite.

"Mom, you make the best creamed spinach," he said, swishing it around in his mouth. "I'm glad most kids hate it."

"You do?" said Mrs. Potter. She patted the side of her hair. "Why?"

Henry grinned. "So that there will be more spinach for me!"

The next morning Henry made up his mind. He was going to ask Rosa to be his valentine. And he was going to do it himself. He just hoped someone else, someone like Billy, hadn't asked her already.

Henry got to class early. Ms. Hatfield was busy pinning valentines on the walls. Ginger Stein was helping her.

Henry walked up to Rosa's desk. She was drawing a heart on a piece of red paper.

As soon as she saw Henry, she covered the paper with her hand.

"Hi," said Henry. "Are you making a valentine?"

43

Henry thought he'd start talking about valentines. Then, when the time was right, he'd ask Rosa the big question. "Why rush right into it?" he thought.

"Yes, I'm making a valentine," said Rosa. She smiled. "For someone special."

"Valentines are fun to make, aren't they?" said Henry.

"How would you know?" said Rosa. "You didn't help us make any yesterday."

Henry gulped. "Sorry," he said.

"We had to decorate the whole place by ourselves," said Rosa. "It wasn't easy. Thanks to you."

Henry sighed. It wasn't going to be easy to ask Rosa the big question. Not right then.

Rosa pointed to the card under her hand. "I'm kind of busy," she said.

"I can see that," said Henry. He looked around the room nervously. "Maybe I better go help Ms. Hatfield."

"Good idea," said Rosa.

"See you later," said Henry.

"See you," said Rosa.

Henry felt lower than a pebble at the bottom of the sea.

"I might as well forget about Rosa," he said. "She's not going to be my valentine. There's no point in even asking."

Henry sighed. He had never been so sad in his life. Slowly, he shuffled toward the front of the room. But when he came to Melvin Purdy's desk he suddenly stopped. Melvin was reading a big red book. Henry looked at the title: *How to Make Someone Like You.*

Henry tapped the book. "Are you studying how to be Cupid?" asked Henry.

Melvin looked up.

"I have to study," he said. "I'm in business!"

"Business?"

Melvin pointed to his paper heart. "You're not the only one who has trouble talking to their valentine," he said. "So far five people have asked me to say nice things to their valentine."

Henry bent down till he was nose to nose with Melvin. He raised an eyebrow and lowered his voice to a whisper. "Has Billy Hayes hired you?"

45

Melvin reached into his back pocket. He pulled out a crinkled-up piece of paper. "Yep," he said, reading from the paper. "Billy is paying me fifty cents to deliver a valentine card."

"I'll pay you a dollar," said Henry desperately. "Work for me instead."

Melvin shook his head. "Sorry, Henry. I have too much business already. Everybody wants help from Cupid."

Henry licked his lips and looked at Melvin's book.

"Is that a good book?"

Melvin knocked on the cover with his fist. "It's the best," he said. "The author guarantees that he can make people like each other."

"Really?" said Henry. He was dying to peek inside the book.

"Can we talk later?" said Melvin. "I've got a lot of reading to do. And not much time to do it in."

"I'm desperate," said Henry. He shot a look at Rosa. "Valentine's is only two days away. And so is my birthday."

Melvin shook his head. "Sorry," he said. "Cupid's time is all filled up."

Henry was getting ready to beg when Ms. Hatfield suddenly clapped her hands.

"Seats, everyone," she said.

Henry took a last look at Melvin's book and walked slowly back to his desk.

"I bet that book is filled with magic words," said Henry. "If only I knew what they were. Then all I'd have to do is say them. And abracadabra, Rosa would be my valentine."

Chapter 6

◆

Talking Milk

"Happy two-days-before-Valentine's," said Ms. Hatfield after everyone had taken their seats.

"Happy two-days-before-my-birthday," said Henry. "Have you all been shopping for my present?" He turned around and waved to the class. "Hint, hint."

Henry wanted everyone to say, "Yes. We're planning a big party with a chocolate cake and lots of presents." But that isn't what they said. In fact, the class didn't say anything. They just laughed.

"Some friends," said Henry, moping.

Ms. Hatfield was wearing her Wednesday

tennis shoes. Low tops, covered with blue and yellow flowers. She peered over her glasses at Henry.

"I'm sure you'll have a very nice birthday," she said.

Henry chewed on his thumb. He wished Ms. Hatfield were right. But he knew different. On Friday everyone would only be thinking about valentines.

Ms. Hatfield smiled. "This morning we're going to talk about etiquette. Who knows what that means?"

"Is it something to eat?" asked Melvin.

"No," said Ms. Hatfield. "Anyone else?"

"Is it a country?" asked Rosa.

"No," said Ms. Hatfield. "*Etiquette* means proper manners. Like asking to be excused from the table. Or writing a thank-you note when someone sends you a present."

Ms. Hatfield began writing a list of good manners on the board. But Henry didn't pay any attention. His mind was on Melvin's book. "I wish Melvin would let me borrow that book," he thought. "I bet it's filled with great secrets. Things you can do to trick people into liking you."

49

Suddenly, Henry heard Ms. Hatfield say, "If someone has helped you out, or if you are going to ask someone for a favor, then it's sometimes nice to bring them a gift. That's good etiquette."

"My mom did that," said Rosa, raising her hand. "She took some flowers to our neighbor, Mrs. Porter. That's because she is going to make us a cake."

"I hope it's a chocolate cake," said Henry. He wiggled his eyebrows. "Hint, hint."

Rosa rolled her eyes. "It's not for you," she said.

Henry frowned. But what Ms. Hatfield had said gave him an idea.

"I know how to get Rosa to like me," he said to himself. "I'll give her a gift."

When lunchtime came Henry hurried to the cafeteria. Along the way he passed Melvin Purdy. Melvin sniffed the air. Then turned to Henry.

"Chocolate milk," he said.

"Wonderful," said Henry. He knew that Rosa liked chocolate milk. "Perhaps good etiquette will make Rosa my valentine yet."

Henry stepped into the cafeteria and

looked around. Rosa was sitting in a corner of the room with Ginger and the other Creepy Creatures. The place was packed. He spotted Billy Hayes a moment later. His orange hat stood out in the crowd like a flashing neon sign. He was with Angie. They were in line for the day's lunch, macaroni and cheese.

"What a goofball," said Henry. He shook his head. "How can Rosa like him?"

Henry got in the back of the line. He was hungry. He got a plateful of macaroni and cheese. Then he got an extra-big cup of chocolate milk.

"You must be very thirsty," said Mrs. Ames. She had a new heart pinned to her cook's hat. This one said: WHAT'S COOKING, BABY?

"This milk isn't for me," said Henry. "It's a gift. I'm going to ask someone special to be my valentine."

Mrs. Ames smiled. "Ahhh. Isn't that nice," she said.

"I hope she says yes," said Henry.

"Don't worry. My chocolate milk is special. It's sure to win her heart," said Mrs. Ames.

"I hope you're right," said Henry. "I'm counting on this milk to help me say the words I have to say."

"The milk makes a nice gift. But speak for yourself," said Mrs. Ames. "If you let something else do the talking, you never know what it might say." She nodded. "That's good advice. In fact, I just told Billy Hayes the same thing."

Henry's mouth fell open. "You did?" He spun around and looked out into the cafeteria. There was Billy. His orange hat was bobbing along through the crowd. And he was heading right for Rosa's table!

"Is Billy going to give his valentine chocolate milk?" asked Henry.

"Yes, indeed," said Mrs. Ames. "He seemed so excited."

Henry gulped. He had to stop Billy before he could get to Rosa. And he had to get there quick.

"Isn't Valentine's wonderful," said Mrs. Ames. She folded her hands and put them under her chin. She closed her eyes. "Love is in the air. Cupid is on the wing."

And a moment later so was Henry.

Balancing his tray with one hand, clearing people out of the way with the other, he raced toward Rosa's table.

Blam! He brushed the back of a tall sixth grader. Some of the milk sloshed out of the cup.

"Hey! Watch where you're going!" shouted the boy.

Henry didn't even slow down. He had more important things on his mind.

"Billy is almost to Rosa," said Henry. He ducked and went under the outstretched arms of Mr. Dean and Mrs. Horton. They had been standing in the aisle, shaking hands.

"Gangway!" said Henry. He skidded around two girls, juggled the tray, and raced off again. The milk sloshed. The plate of macaroni bounced up and down as if it were on springs.

Billy was just behind Rosa when Henry finally caught up.

"Rosa!" yelled Henry, barreling down the aisle.

Billy stopped and turned. Rosa swiveled in her chair.

Henry yelled. "Rosa! Wait! I got something for you."

Rosa opened her mouth to speak. But the words never had a chance to come out.

"Whoa ... Ohhh ... Ohhhhh!" yelled Henry, slipping. He was pitching forward, coming toward Rosa like a rocket. An out-of-control one. Desperately, he tried to get his balance. But it was too late. "Whoa ... Ohhhh ... noooooo...." Arms and legs churning, he started to go down. The tray went flying.

Rosa shrieked. So did everyone else at the table, all the Creepy Creatures.

The milk and the macaroni shot through the air. For a moment everyone froze. Then ... SPLAT!

Half the mess plowed right into Rosa. The rest splattered onto the Creepy Creatures.

Henry skidded onto the milky floor. But he jumped up right away when he saw Rosa blast out of her chair. She was a dripping, milky mess. A gob of macaroni, like a tiny sled, came sliding down her nose.

"Excuse me," said Henry. Trying to be polite. Trying to show the proper etiquette.

Rosa plucked a piece of macaroni from her ear. She looked madder than anything. She stomped her foot into a puddle of milk. "Henry Potter! Sometimes ... sometimes ..."

Henry began backing away. "Accidents happen," he said.

Rosa shook her head. "But why do they only happen when you're around?"

Henry kept backing away. "This is probably a bad time to ask Rosa to be my valentine," he thought. He shot a look at Billy. Like everyone else he was standing with his mouth open. Everything had happened so fast, he didn't know what to do.

Someone started to laugh. Then another and another. Soon everyone in the cafeteria was laughing and pointing. The Creepy Creatures, soaked with macaroni and milk, had never been so embarrassed. Rosa pulled a gob of gooey cheese out of her hair and narrowed her eyes.

"Go!" she said, pointing at Henry.

Henry didn't have to be asked twice. He

took off like a poked rabbit. Out the door and down the hall he ran. He didn't stop till he was nearly back to the classroom. Then, leaning up against a locker, he caught his breath and said to himself, "Mom was right. So was Mrs. Ames. I should have spoken for myself. Instead I let the chocolate milk do the talking. And I'm afraid Rosa didn't like what the milk had to say."

Chapter 7

◆

Hint, Hint

On Thursday morning Ms. Hatfield said, "Happy one-day-before-Valentine's-Day."

"Happy one-day-before-Valentine's," the class said back.

Ms. Hatfield smiled at Henry. "And happy one-day-before-Henry's-birthday too," she added.

"Thank you," said Henry. He stood up and pressed down the feather of hair sticking up in back. If he was going to have a big party, like the one in the picture, he would have to remind everyone about his big day. "Remember, my friends. Only one shopping day left till my birthday," he shouted.

Everyone laughed. Except for Ginger Stein.

She whispered from the back of the room. "I'd like to get you a present, all right. Some macaroni and milk, delivered to your face."

Henry turned around and waved. "Sorry," he said.

Ginger put her fingers in her ears and stuck out her tongue.

"I have a feeling Ginger isn't going to give me a big party," he said.

After school Henry walked home by himself. In the next block he could see Rosa, Melvin, and Ginger. Ginger's red curls were shining in the sun like a bright little fire. Normally he would have been walking with them. But he didn't think they wanted to see him. Not after what had happened the day before.

It was a bright and sunny afternoon. But to Henry it felt cold and dreary. He kicked a rock and sent it skittering into the gutter.

He turned down River Street. He went past the Lucky Laundromat, Mason's Gifts, and Cricket's Bookshop. He was just about to walk by the Happy Time Party Shop

when he saw Melvin, Rosa, and Ginger standing inside.

"I bet they're getting stuff for the Valentine's party," he said. "I wonder if they could use some help?"

Henry put his face to the window and looked inside. Melvin was wearing a funny pointed hat. He was dancing around in the aisle. Ginger and Rosa were watching him and giggling.

Henry sighed. "It looks like they're having fun."

Just then Rosa looked up and saw Henry's nose pressed against the glass. She gasped and waved for him to leave. Ginger and Melvin picked up some things from a shelf. Then they ran down the aisle and disappeared.

"Go, go," Rosa was saying. Henry couldn't hear her words. But he could read her lips.

"I guess she's still mad," he thought.

Henry was trying to decide whether to go in, when Melvin walked out the door. He touched Henry on the arm and said, "Come on. I'll walk home with you."

"Why can't we walk home with Ginger and Rosa?" asked Henry.

"Because," said Melvin. He nodded. "You know."

"Are they still mad?" asked Henry.

"A little," said Melvin. "But everyone will be fine by tomorrow at the party." He tugged on Henry's sleeve. "Come on. Let's go."

Henry took one last look through the window. Ginger and Rosa were peeking at him from behind some shelves. When they saw him look, they yanked their heads back.

Henry sighed. "They're acting like I'm a monster or something."

"Maybe they're afraid you're going to get them again with milk and macaroni," said Melvin. He grinned. "Accidents happen, you know."

"Don't I know," said Henry.

Chapter 8

◆

Cupid Knows Best

Henry and Melvin walked down River Street in silence. Finally, Melvin blew on his fingers. Then he rubbed them on his little paper heart.

"Cupid strikes again," he said. "Guess who is Ginger's valentine?"

Henry grinned. "Is it you?"

"Yep," said Melvin. He puffed out his chest. "I asked her after school. And she said yes."

Henry looked down at Melvin. He was the littlest, scaredest kid in the Creepy Creature Club. But at that moment he seemed like the bravest man in the world.

"How did you ask her?" said Henry. "What did you say?" He winked. "I bet you used a trick from your book. Right?"

They stopped under a tall, leafless tree. Melvin nodded. "I did use a trick. You're right."

Henry leaned in close. "What trick was it? Tell me, please. I'm desperate."

"The trick, if you can call it a trick, was honesty," said Melvin.

Henry put his hands on his hips. "Honesty?"

"Yep, the book said the best way to make friends is to be honest with them. So I was," said Melvin.

"So, what did you say?" asked Henry.

"I asked her what I really wanted to know," said Melvin. "I was honest. I said, 'Ginger, will you be my valentine?' Those were my exact words."

"And she said yes?"

"Yes!" said Melvin. "It was so easy." He patted the little heart. "Maybe I really am Cupid."

Henry shook his head. "I wish I could be as brave as you. But I can't. I get scared

just thinking about asking Rosa to be my valentine."

"What are you afraid of?" said Melvin.

"I'm afraid she'll say no," said Henry. "Think about it. I'm big, brave Henry Potter. I'm the best at everything. If she said no I'd be so embarrassed, I'd turn purple."

Melvin put his hand on Henry's arm. "If you never ask you'll never know. Rosa doesn't want to embarrass you. Nobody does. It would be bad manners. Bad etiquette, says Ms. Hatfield."

Henry nodded. "Rosa does have good manners. I guess that's one of the reasons I like her."

"Promise me that you'll ask Rosa to be your valentine tomorrow morning," said Melvin. "First thing in the morning, before school starts."

Henry narrowed his eyes. "What about Billy Hayes?"

"What about him?" said Melvin.

"I thought Cupid was going to help him get a valentine," said Henry.

"Cupid is," said Melvin. "Tomorrow. After

school. Cupid is going to shoot his little arrow for Billy."

"Then I better talk to Rosa in the morning," said Henry.

"The sooner the better," said Melvin. "That's another thing my book says. Don't put things off."

"I won't," said Henry. He gave Melvin a tap on the shoulder. "If you can do it, so can I."

"Take it from me, the expert," said Melvin. He patted his little paper heart. "Believe me. Cupid knows best."

Chapter 9

◆

Happy Birthday to You

Friday morning. It was Valentine's Day and Henry's birthday all rolled into one. Ms. Hatfield had on a special pair of tennis shoes. White ones. High tops. Covered with little red hearts.

"Happy Valentine's Day!" she said. During the week so many valentines had been put up that the walls were red.

"Happy Valentine's!" said the class. Everyone had on something red.

Henry looked across the aisle at Rosa. "Happy Valentine's," he said.

"Happy Valentine's," said Rosa. Henry had never seen her looking so pretty. She had a red bow in her hair. She was wearing a fluffy pink dress. She grinned. "I hope you're coming to the Valentine's party."

Henry nodded. "Hint, hint. Is there anything else you want to say besides happy Valentine's?"

Rosa scratched her chin. "Good morning?"

"Hint, hint," said Henry. "Chocolate cake and ice cream. Lots of presents. Candles!"

"Christmas dinner?" said Rosa.

"No. It's my—"

"Shhhhh!" went Ms. Hatfield. She put her finger near her lips. "Talking in class is bad etiquette."

Henry nodded. What a horrible birthday this was turning out to be. First Rosa doesn't remember his birthday. Then he gets in trouble for talking.

He reached back and took the picture of the birthday party out of his pocket. He stretched his legs out under the desk and studied the picture.

"What a lucky kid," muttered Henry. "He's having the happiest birthday ever." He folded up the picture and returned it to his pocket. "Poor me. I'll never have a birthday like his." He sighed. "Maybe I was just born on the wrong day."

Up in front Ms. Hatfield was remembering her favorite Valentine's Day.

"I was in the third grade," she said. "Six people asked me to be their valentine and I said yes to every one of them." She laughed. "That was my favorite Valentine's Day." She looked around the room. "Who wants to tell us about their favorite day?"

Lots of people raised their hands. But not Henry. He couldn't remember his favorite Valentine's. All he could remember was his worst Valentine's. The one he was having that very day.

While everyone was telling their story Henry practiced what he was going to say to Rosa at lunch.

"Rosa, will you be my valentine?" He said it over and over in his head. It seemed so easy. Just six honest little words. But he still thought they were the scariest six words in the world.

When the bell rang for lunch he was ready.

"Time is running out," he said. "I have to ask her. Now."

Henry took a deep breath and stood up. The class was hurrying out the door. He drew in a deep breath, turned to face Rosa's desk. And discovered she was gone.

Henry turned to Melvin. He was wearing red pants. As usual they were too short. "Did you see Rosa leave?" asked Henry.

"She was the first one out the door," said Melvin. His tiny eyes sparkled. "Did you ask her to be your valentine?"

Henry shook his head. "I'll ask her in the cafeteria."

"No, you won't," said Melvin. They began walking toward the door.

"No. This time I will. I've made up my mind," said Henry.

"What I meant was that you can't," said Melvin. "Rosa got permission to go home early. Her mother came to meet her. They're going to get ready for the party."

The hallway was filled with students. Everyone was laughing and talking as they headed for lunch. Henry was waiting for Melvin to wish him a happy birthday. But

he didn't. All he could talk about was Valentine's.

"Ms. Hatfield said I was the best Cupid she'd ever seen," said Melvin. "This week was fun. I liked helping people become friends."

Henry nodded. "Hint, hint," he said. "Chocolate cake and ice cream. Candles and presents."

When Melvin didn't take the hint, Henry started humming the song "Happy Birthday to You." But even that didn't get his attention. So Henry started singing the song. Loud.

"Henry, please," said Melvin at last. "It's rude to sing when someone is talking. It's poor etiquette. Ms. Hatfield says so."

Henry stopped. He put his hands on his hips. "And it's rude to forget someone's birthday too."

Melvin drew back his head. "Whose birthday is it?"

Henry rolled his eyes. "Mine, of course."

Melvin snapped his fingers. "That's right. Happy birthday."

"It hasn't been very happy," said Henry. "I wish someone would remember."

Melvin patted Henry on the arm. "It's Valentine's Day," he said. "People are thinking about other things."

"You would think my friends would remember," said Henry. "What's a club for, anyway?"

"For parties," said Melvin. "Come to the clubhouse after school. You'll feel better."

Henry nodded. "I will feel better," he said. "But the Creepy Creatures won't. Not when they get the surprise I'm going to give them."

Chapter 10

♦

The Valentine's Party

The whole rest of the day not one person wished Henry a happy birthday. By the time school was out he wasn't upset anymore. Instead he was mad. Real mad.

Head down, he stomped all the way to Rosa's garage.

"The Creepy Creatures need to learn some etiquette," he said. "And I'm going to give them the lesson. Melvin is right. There's nothing like honesty to get your point across."

When Henry got to the clubhouse he saw a big red heart on the door. It said,

HAPPY HAUNTED VALENTINE'S. Music was coming from inside. It was scary organ music.

Henry took a deep breath and opened the door.

The clubhouse was jammed. Everyone was talking and laughing. Suddenly the music stopped.

Rosa had turned off the tape player. She pointed at Henry and yelled, "Look, everybody. It's Henry!"

"Yes, it is!" shouted Henry before anyone could say another word. "And you're going to listen to what I say no matter what."

"We always do anyhow!" shouted someone.

Henry frowned. "You people have the worst manners in River City. You're lucky I haven't quit and joined the Sharks."

"What makes you think we'd let you join?" someone shouted. Henry squinted out into the crowd. He shaded his eyes with his hand. It was Billy Hayes. He would have recognized that goofy orange hat and that stupid through-the-nose voice anywhere. Angie Dobbs was standing next to him, drinking some punch. "What are they doing here?" he wondered.

Henry took a deep breath and went on. "You all need lessons in etiquette!" he shouted.

"Good advice," yelled a familiar voice. He looked over by the punch bowl. It was Ms. Hatfield. What was she doing at the party?

"Nobody even wished me a happy birthday," said Henry.

"Happy birthday!" shouted everyone.

Henry dismissed them with a wave. "Too late," he said. "You should have been nicer during the week. You had your chance."

"But, Henry," yelled Rosa. "Henry—"

"And one more thing," said Henry. "Rosa, I want to talk to you. There's something I got to say. And I don't care what you say back."

It was time to be honest. Time to speak up. Henry was so mad, he never even stopped to think about being scared.

"Rosa! Will you be my valentine?"

The room suddenly became quiet as a tomb.

Rosa stood up straight.

"Well?" said Henry.

Rosa nodded. She chewed on a strand of her long black hair. "How can I stay mad at someone as silly as Henry?" she muttered. "He's one of a kind."

"I've been trying to ask you all week, but something always went wrong," said Henry. "But now I'm asking you right out. In person. Rosa, will you be my valentine?"

Rosa shut her eyes. She took a deep breath, then opened her eyes. "Yes," she whispered. "I'll be your valentine, Henry Potter."

Henry beamed. He put his hands on his hips and looked out at the crowd. Standing right under the big rubber spider was a tall woman in a cook's hat. It was Mrs. Ames. The valentine on her hat said: YOU'RE MY SWEET POTATO! And next to her was another woman he knew. The woman had sparkling round glasses. She was patting her hair. She was his mom! "What are they doing here?" he wondered.

"Thanks to Rosa I just got the best birthday present ever," said Henry. He pointed out at the crowd. "None of the rest of you even remembered that today was my birthday." He sneered. "Thanks a lot!"

Suddenly Henry felt someone tugging on his sleeve. He looked down. It was Melvin.

"Would you calm down and look around?" said Melvin. "Can't you see?"

Henry stuck out his neck and squinted. The big rubber spider was still swinging over the couch. The monster posters were still on the walls. There were some balloons and big hearts hanging from the ceiling. And on the wall there was a big banner.

Henry's mouth fell open. HAPPY BIRTHDAY TO OUR FAVORITE BRAGGER, it said.

That was him!

"Surprise!" everyone yelled.

Henry put his hand on his cheek. He couldn't believe it. No wonder everyone was there, the Sharks, Ms. Hatfield, his mom, and his whole class too.

Then all at once everyone began singing "Happy Birthday to You."

Now Henry put both hands on his cheeks. While everyone sang, Rosa came walking through the crowd carrying a big birthday

cake. It was shaped like a heart. The candles flickered and cast a pretty glow across her face.

Henry beamed.

"You almost found out about the surprise yesterday," said Rosa. "Remember when you saw us in the store? We were buying birthday decorations."

Henry looked at Rosa. Then at Melvin. "I thought you were going to help Billy make Rosa his valentine. What happened?"

Melvin scratched his head. "Billy and Rosa. That isn't what I was going to do."

"But I thought—"

Melvin said, "Billy wanted me to ask Angie for him."

"Did you?"

"I told Billy the same thing I told you. Speak for yourself. Be honest."

"Did he?"

"Yep," said Melvin. "They're valentines." He patted his little heart. "Thanks to Cupid."

Henry looked at Rosa. He felt like the luckiest valentine in the world. "I'm glad I finally spoke up. Melvin was right. It was so easy. I'm only sorry it took so long."

"Me too," said Rosa. "I've been waiting for you to ask me all week."

"Really?" said Henry. "Why didn't you ask me? That sure would have made things easier."

Rosa blushed. She lowered her head. "I was afraid you'd say no. I thought you didn't like me, because you were being so mean."

Henry shook his head. "I wasn't being mean. Only dumb."

"From now on I hope both of you are brave enough to speak for yourself," said Melvin.

"You don't have to worry about me," said Henry. He thumped his fist against his chest. "I'm going to be the bravest, most honest speaker in the world."

Rosa laughed and held out the cake. "Why don't you put that big mouth of yours to a good use?" she said. "Blow out the candles."

Everyone pushed in close.

"Make a wish," said Billy Hayes. He had a red paper heart hanging from his cap. Angie was wearing a paper heart, too, pinned to her dress.

Henry closed his eyes. He made a wish. Then he blew out all the candles with one giant *Whoosh!*

Everyone clapped. "Happy birthday to you," they sang.

"What did you wish?" asked Melvin.

"I wished that all my Valentine's Days will be as happy as this one," he said.

"Ahhhh," said Mrs. Ames. She folded her hands and put them under her chin. "Isn't Valentine's great?"

Rosa and Henry exchanged glances. They couldn't have agreed with Mrs. Ames more. Henry felt wonderful. The party was just like the one in the picture. Maybe even better.

Angie cut the cake.

Mrs. Ames went, "Ahhhh."

So did Henry.

The cake was chocolate.

Monster Jokes

Hi! It's Melvin Purdy again. I've been having so much fun making people like each other that I can't stop. That's why I want to share some of my favorite monster jokes. Pass these on to someone you know. If you can make them laugh, they'll be a friend for life.

Cupid guarantees it.

Why did Dr. Frankenstein say his son's grades were all underwater?
Because they were all below C-level.

What did the grapes say when the giant stepped on them?
Nothing, they just let out a little whine.

What would you call a dragon who ate his mom's sister?
An aunt-eater.

Why are all skeletons cowards?
They don't have any guts.

Zombie Joe: Where did you get that nice tie?
Zombie Moe: Oh it's just a little something I dug up.

Will: What would you do if Dracula and the Swamp Monster came to your door?
Bill: Hope it was Halloween.

Dracula: Did you hear the news? Dr. Frankenstein just gave the invisible man a job.
Werewolf: I don't know what he sees in him.

What job did the ghost get on the basketball team?
He was the team spirit.

In what part of the house will you never find a zombie?
In the living room.

Knock-knock
Who's there?
Tank
Tank who?
Tank you for listening to these silly jokes.